The House That Time Forgot

Cover art: Shutterstock/Taisiya Kozorez

Cover design: Jennifer Do

10 9 8 7 6 5 4 3 2 1

ISBN 979-8-8809-1657-3

The House That Time Forgot

Robert F. Young

Nodding in the wing-back chair before the brightly blazing fire, she heard the flapping again—the dismal sweep of leathery tissue against stagnant overheated air. "Come," she said, I know you don't like me, but you are my guests you know, so the very least you can do is reveal yourselves and sit down and keep me company while you're deciding how to dispose of me,"

She had a hunch that her hospitality disconcerted them, because no sooner had she spoken than the flapping faded away. Probably, she reflected, they were accustomed to people who shivered in their shoes at the mere thought of death, or maybe they were so used to being hated that not being hated hurt their feelings. No doubt it was difficult for them to go about their dirty work in a congenial atmosphere.

Opening her eyes, she regarded the emptiness of the room. When you live in emptiness long enough, you can see it. Elizabeth Dickenson could, anyway. Of recent years she had become quite an expert in the field of emptiness. She put on the horn-rimmed spectacles which, when her eyes had started to go bad, she had resurrected from an old chest that had once belonged to her grandmother. They didn't entirely correct her presbyopia, but they were better than no spectacles at all. Picking up the book she had been reading, she chose a page at random and let her eyes rest briefly on its all-too-familiar words—

The face of all the world is changed, I think,
Since first I heard the footsteps of thy soul
Move still, oh, still, beside me, as they stole
Betwixt me and the dreadful outer brink
Of obvious death, where I, who thought to sink,
Was caught up into love.

Wearily, she closed the book and let it drop to the floor beside her chair. She removed her spectacles and laid them on the yellow lap robe which she had drawn over her legs. She had heard *his* footsteps in the dim and distant future, and had let them go unanswered. She had never heard them again.

Flap-fiap! went the melancholy wings.

THE HOUSE THAT TIME FORGOT

She returned her gaze to the emptiness of the room. All of the furniture was gone now except her chair and her footstool, and her spool bed upstairs; but the emptiness had been there even when the rest of the furniture was present. In the beginning, she had sold the various pieces to pay her taxes; after that, she had burned them to keep warm. She had burned her books, too—save for the one that lay beside the chair. As for her bridges, she had burned them long ago. Now that the house had finally found itself, plenty of cordwood was available, but she couldn't order cordwood and expect to pay for it by means of a checking account that hadn't come into existence yet, and the same objection applied to the trees that stood in the yard. Presumably, she owned them, but she could hardly burn them in the fireplace or in the wood stove without first hiring someone to cut them down and saw and split them into appropriate dimensions. And besides, even assuming that she could manage to keep from freezing to death, what was to keep her from starving to death after her meager food-supply gave out? No wonder the obbly-gobblies had come!

On the mantel, a clock without hands stood. None of the other clocks in Elizabeth's house had had hands either, before they disappeared. As for calendars, she had dispensed with them almost from the start. In a way, the house was more of a time-ship than it was a house—a time-ship in which she had set sail for the islands of the past. But the sea of time had turned out to be a dark and treacherous river, and the river had been unkind. Equally as distressing, rats of memory had crawled on board before she had cast off, and down through the years she had heard them scrabbling in the darkness of long and lonely nights. But the obbly-gobblies were going to change all that. She liked the obbly- gobblies, Elizabeth Dickenson did.

The dismal flapping of their wings had faded away again. But she knew that they were still in the room. She could sense their presence. What were they waiting for? she wondered. She had known the minute she first heard them in the house that they had come to do her in. Why, then, did they not get on with the grisly task and have done with it? She leaned back in the wing-back chair and closed her eyes. The flapping intensified. *Now I lay me down to sleep,* she thought, *I pray the obbly-gobblies my soul to keep. And if I die before I wake, I Pray the obbly-globblies my soul to take . . .*

*

The house had an interesting history. In the phase we are concerned with here (in a different phase he was to build it), Theodore Dickenson discovered it when he came to Sweet Clover in 1882 to establish the Dickenson Grain-Machinery Company, and he fell in love with it at first sight. It was large and Victorian and built of red brick, and it stood all alone about a quarter of a mile outside the village on a dirt road that would someday be known as Linden Street. On the first floor there was a spacious living room, a huge library, a majestic dining room, a commodious kitchen, and a compact pantry; on the second floor there were six big bedrooms. The cellar was roomy and dry, and the untouched grounds—there was neither driveway nor walk—would lend themselves readily to landscaping.

Upon making inquiries with a view to purchasing the place, Theodore learned a number of disconcerting facts: all of the villagers were familiar enough with the house, but none of them could remember who had built it, or when; apparently no one had lived in it for years, a circumstance which strongly suggested, to the majority of the villagers at least, that it was haunted; in the absence of either owner or heirs, the village of Sweet Clover had legally confiscated it and was eager to sell it for a song, provided the buyer could pay cash. Needless to say, this final fact was not nearly as disconcerting as the two previous ones, and Theodore, the recent recipient of a deceased uncle's modest fortune, wasted no time in taking advantage of the opportunity. He bought the house, plus a large lot on either side, and shortly afterward moved in with his wife Ann. They went to work immediately on the desolate and dingy place, hiring painters, masons, and carpenters to refurbish it inside and out. Generally speaking, Victorian furniture was already losing its popularity in the year 1882, but in small towns like Sweet Clover it was still very much in vogue. Accordingly, Theodore and Ann furnished the entire house with the best Victorian pieces they could buy, supplementing them with *objects d'art* endemic to the era. Out of sentimentalism they retained the several pieces that had come with the house, and refinished them with loving care. In addition Theodore bought an imported harpsichord, hoping that his wife would take up music. Ann, however, gave the instrument a wide berth, and it was left all to itself in an unfrequented corner of the living room, there to gather dust and desuetude.

The Dickenson Grain Machinery Company, let it be said forthwith, was left to gather neither. Under Theodore's shrewd generalship and despite the depression then in progress, the factory grew from an infantile sprawl of shed-like structures into a proud young plant and brought a prosperity to Sweet Clover such as the little town had never known. In 1888, as though by way of reward, Ann bore him a son, whom they named Nelson and whom Theodore began grooming to take over the business almost from the moment the child began to walk. This process continued through puberty and adolescence, and meanwhile DGM survived three more depressions and matured into one of the most stable firms in the state.

Nelson turned out to be as shrewd a businessman as his father. In 1917, he married Nora James, a reticent girl two years his senior , but, as Theodore put it, "of good aristocratic stock." It was said around Sweet Clover that the main reason Nelson married her was to enhance his chances of not being conscripted under the newly-enacted Selective Service Act, but this was unjust to say in the least. Had Theodore desired to, he could have kept all of the young men in Sweet Clover out of the army, to say nothing of his own son. In any event, Nelson did not go to war, and in 1919, when his father died suddenly of a stroke, he took over both the House of Dickenson (as it was now referred to by the villagers) and DGM. A few months later, his mother died, bringing to a close a way of life that had endured in the house for thirty-seven years.

But only partly to a close. Nelson had inherited both his father's and his mother's sentimentalism, and as a result he was reluctant to disturb the atmosphere of their somewhat antiquated way of living. At the same time he was reluctant to go on staying in the house without investing it with some evidence of his own existence. Theodore and Ann had resisted change insofar as it involved furniture, and for the most part the House of Dickenson was still furnished with the same Victorian pieces they had bought when they first moved in. These pieces, however, had never been allowed to fall into disrepair, and, well-built to begin with, were in as good condition now as they had been originally. Nelson loved them, each and everyone, but fortunately or unfortunately, as the case may be—there was a limit to his love. New furniture was being manufactured every day, and he and Nora certainly had as much right to buy it as their less encumbered neighbors did. Moreover, there was no real reason why they shouldn't: it was perfectly possible to bring in the new and still retain the old, provided you used a reasonable amount of good taste and provided you weren't afraid to be a little bit unconventional. So he and Nora began replacing some, although by no means all, of the Victorian pieces with post-WW I furniture, in each case blending in the new with the old to the maximum extent possible. The result, when they completed the project, both surprised and enchanted them. Here was not heterogeneity, but charm—the charm of two worlds tied tastefully and unobstrusively together.

In 1920, Nora gave birth to a son whom they named Byron, after her favorite poet. Byron, too, turned out to be an only child, but here any and all similarity to his father ended and similarity to his namesake began. He even looked like George Gordon, Lord Byron; certainly, he acted like him. In fact, the only thing that disqualified him for total identification was his disinclination to write poetry. Possibly it was this sole dis similarity that heartened Nelson; in any event, despite the depression years that presently came along he saw to it that his son learned . everything there was to know about the anatomy of DGM. WW II interfered considerably with his over all plans, but did not completely dash them to the ground. Byron, as might have been expected, became a war hero; he also, as might have been expected, became involved in a fly-by-night wartime marriage that resulted in a baby girl whose custody became his and his alone when, at the end of the war, his wife left the child in a basket at the gate of the separation center where he was being processed for discharge and ran off with another man. Undaunted,

THE HOUSE THAT TIME FORGOT

Byron brought the child to the House of Dickenson and dared his parents not to love and adore it as much as he did, after which he settled down grimly and went to work at DGM, channeling his wild ways into souping up specimens of the new cars that presently began appearing on the post-war scene.

*

The child's name was Elizabeth. From the beginning she was shy and sensitive, and, except for her father's, preferred no one's company to her own. Her father, she revered, It was not surprising that, living in an atmosphere predominated by antique furniture, Currier & Ives prints, and grandfather's clocks, she should come to prefer the old to the new; nor was it surprising that she should insist on taking lessons on the harpsichord which still stood in its unfrequented corner in the living room. She took to Bach the way a duck takes to water, and she came to love both Couperin and Scarlatti. Music, however, was far from being the major passion in her young life. She had begun to read almost as soon as she had begun to talk, and at the age of nine she had penned her first poem. Twelve found her with the three heroines who were to remain with her down through the years and upon one of those lives she was to model her own: Elizabeth Barrett Browning, Christina Georgina Rossetti, and Emily Dickinson. Laughingly—and lovingly—her father bestowed upon her the nickname of "Elizabeth Georgina Dickinson."

Byron did his level best at DGM, but it was obvious from the beginning that he had inherited neither his father's nor his grandfather's business acumen. However, this did not prevent him from inheriting the factory when, in the summer of '60, both Nelson and Nora drowned when Nelson's cruiser capsized in an abrupt Lake Erie storm. Byron and sixteen-year old Elizabeth sat solemnly through church services and afterward stood solemnly in the cemetery beneath the tent that shrouded the two caskets, and when it was all over they rode solemnly back to the large and empty house. But neither of them grieved long. Byron had DGM on his shoulders now, and the unaccustomed responsibility sapped his mental and physical energies to a degree where all else seemed unreal; and as for Elizabeth, while she had loved her grandparents, the major part of her love had been—and still was—focused on her father, and she found that she could not carry her regret over their passing beyond penning a long poem in their memory. The poem finished, she penned others about more immediate subjects, and soon the summer was over and she was off to finishing school.

She had never liked regular school, and she liked finishing school even less. For one thing, it deprived her of the privacy she had come to take for granted in the House of Dickenson. There, her room had been her *sanctum, sanctorum,* and having to share a room with two other girls was repugnant to her. However, she put up with it as best she could, penning her poetry in the dark with the aid of a small pocket torch which she flicked on after getting into bed and pulling the blankets up over her head. She wrote brief, sensitive stanzas for the most part, imagining them to be in the manner of Emily Dickinson. *Happiness,* she wrote one night—

I came upon you of a summer's day
When I was dancing with my shadow.

*

In the summer of '62, she met Matthew Pearson, the young engineer whom her father had hired to expedite production at DGM. Although young with reference to his profession, he was still ten years older than Elizabeth, and while he was an eligible enough bachelor, he wasn't at all the sort of person someone who didn't know her very well would have dreamed she would fall in love with. Nevertheless, fall in love with him, she did. It was her first love, and her last, and she commemorated it on the very night of their meeting' with the lines,

Breasting life's foothills I came upon him standing in the sun.
I had seen his eyes in the azure of autumn skies;
I had seen his hair in the, blackness of winter woods.
Autumn, winter—father-seasons
Spring, I would bend thine ear!

THE HOUSE THAT TIME FORGOT

For some time, things had been going badly at DGM. Since settling down after the wax, Byron had kept his wildness steadfastly channeled into the driving of faster and faster automobiles, and recently he had found an ideal outlet for it in the racing of his new Ferrari in the hills beyond the town. But a Tack of wildness does not necessarily imply a good business head, and Byron was but little more adept in industrial strategy now than he had been the first day he had taken DGM over. The company was a victim of technological change. Before Byron hired Matthew Pearson on the recommendation of Curtis Hannock, the company's lawyer, every operation was performed precisely as it had been performed in Nelson Dickenson's day, and as a result, the factory was unable to compete with its modernized cousins. The necessary changes should have been instituted ten years ago, and brought about gradually; the fact that they had not been was owing not so much to Nelson's inclination to cling to old, traditional ways as it was to Byron's failure to lend the initiative and to come up with the new ideas which the situation had required. Now, the changes needed to be made all at once, and the company's finances were unequal to the expense. Matthew Pearson had been able to expedite operations somewhat, but, as Byron refused to act on Curtis Hannock's advice to borrow enough money to buy and install the necessary new equipment, the firm had to limp along as best it could, picking up whatever contracts its competitors dropped in their eagerness to snag larger and more lucrative ones. The limp was rapidly becoming a shamble, more and more employees were being laid off, and Byron could be seen racing his Ferrari in the hills at more and more frequent intervals.

Elizabeth's romance with Matthew Pearson, a one-sided affair at first, with one party penning inspired imagery and the other party totally unaware of the affair's existence, kindled suddenly into a full-fledge flame. This came about when Matthew called at the House of Dickenson one evening to discuss a contemplated changeover at the plant with Byron. Quite by accident, he happened to be standing at the foot of the open stairway in the living room just as Elizabeth, wearing a girlish white dress, was coming down.

She did not know it, for all her poetic lore, but there are times when, given the light lighting, the right moment, and the right mood, a tall, slender girl with no other claim to beauty than strong yet sensitive features and a natural grace of deportment can undergo a sort of transcendental transfiguration in the eyes of the beholder. It was so now, Matthew Pearson, newly come in out of a dismal rainy night, the warmth of the House of Dickenson rising reassuringly around him, the furniture of the House of Dickenson, its collective charm but little dimmed by the occasional modern atrocities that Byron had inserted here and there, spread out on either hand, saw a vision of loveliness that, however subjective it may have been, was destined to remain with him for the rest of his life.

After that, he became a frequent visitor at the house. What with the production problems that were continually arising at the factory he was never wanting for an excuse, and after he made his intentions known to Elizabeth late in '63, he did not need an excuse. He had never really needed one anyway, had he but known it; but Elizabeth, never demonstrative even in ordinary matters, had kept her love as deep and as dark a secret as she kept the poems she wrote in her room at finishing school. She graduated in the spring of '64, and she and Matthew announced their engagement. The announcement appeared in the *Sweet Clover Gazette* on the same day Byron Dickenson ran his Ferrari into a bridge abutment, impaled himself on the steering column, and neatly sheared off the top of his head.

*

The flowers were the worst. Elizabeth loved wild flowers, but she hated domesticated blooms. She hated the chrysanthemums most of all. There were mums in every bouquet, in every wreath. The floral piece which she had ordered over the phone and which said "DAUGHTER" in ugly gilt letters was thick with them. It should have been woven of violets and forget-me-nots; of gentians and hepaticas and wood-sorrels; of lupines, foxgloves, cinquefoils, and Queen Anne's lace. *How can I say how much I love thee when I have naught but stereotyped words at my command? I need the traceries of morning glories on a summer hill, or the gentle blueness of morning sun. . .*

THE HOUSE THAT TIME FORGOT

It was raining when the line of solemn cars filed into the cemetery, and the casket was set in place in the cement-block shelter which the modern-minded cemetery officials had had constructed in order that death could be consummated with a minimum of discomfort to its beholders. The shelter was painted grass-green, both inside and out, and had a damp, musty smell. People, some of whom had been Byron's friends and some of whom had been his enemies, crowded in and lined up behind the two chairs that stood before the casket. In one of the chairs, Elizabeth sat, in the other, Matthew Pearson. Byron had left friends and enemies, but in addition to his daughter the only relatives he had left was a scattering of cousins who lived too far away to make attending the funeral practicable.

Elizabeth sat silently, listening to the minister intone his time worn words. She had not known about the shelter; she had expected to stand beneath a dripping tent. She would have liked to stand in the rain itself, to have felt it on her face. There was poetry in the rain, solace. Here in the shelter there was only indifference and death.

"—dust to dust—"

No, not dust. My father will never be dust. My father will be the wind. When you drive in the hills at night you will hear his voice. He will speak to you through the rolled-down windows of your cars, and he will say a thousand wondrous things. My father will be the wind! . . .

The flower that the minister had handed her was a chrysanthemum. She stood up and laid it gently on the casket. *This is a bluebell, father. I found it in the meadows south of town. I picked it because it made me think of your eyes—those gentle, understanding eyes that I shall never?" see again—*

Matthew was standing beside her. "Elizabeth, are you all right?"

"Yes." She looked up into his eyes. "Your eyes—they're like bluebells, too."

He took her arm. "Come, Elizabeth. It's time to go."

The House of Dickenson stood silently in the rain. Byron and Elizabeth had dispensed with the regular servants some time ago, and a cleaning woman came twice a week to do the rooms. Matthew helped Elizabeth out of the car and walked with her as far as the front door. "I hate to go running off to the city at a time like this," he said, "but it wouldn't be fair to the company : if I didn't attend the Schwartz and Burghardt auction."

"Why can't you send someone else ?"

"Because there isn't much money to play around with, and I've got to buy exactly what we need. Cheer up—it'll only be for a couple of days."

"Two days," she said. "Two centuries." She essayed a brave smile, almost brought it off. "Well, if you must, you must, I suppose."

"I'll tell you what. I'll ask Mrs. Barton to come over and keep you company. It's not her day to clean, but—"

"You'll do nothing of the sort ! If I want to hear banalities, I'll turn on TV. Go now, quickly. I'm not a little girl."

"All, right. I'll be staying at the Wilton Hotel—if you need me, don't hesitate to call." He kissed her. "Bye"

"Good by," Elizabeth said.

The trouble was, she *was* a little girl . . .

She watched him drive away, then she entered the house and removed her coat and hat. Looking neither to left nor to right, she walked into the living room and climbed the stairs to her room. The windows were raised, and the curtains were wet with rain. The modern little desk on which she wrote her poems and in which she hid them stood forlornly by an antique spool bed that was older than the house itself. Opened on her pillow lay a slender volume that was older than the house, too—*Sonnets by E.B.B.* She sat down on the bed, reached out and touched the faded words— *I lift my heavy heart up solemnly,*

As once Electra held sepulcher urn,
And looking in thine eyes, I overturn
The ashes at thy feet. Behold and see
What a great heap of grief lay hid in me
And how the red wild sparkles dimly burn—

She could cry then. Afternoon darkened to dusk as she lay there on her silken coverlet, and presently night tiptoed into the room. Toward midnight, the rain stopped, and the stars came out. Lying on her back now, she could see them through the window by the bed. She counted the jewels of Orion's belt. She traced the little dog's tail. She marveled at the misted magic of Berenice's hair. At long last, she slept.

*

The answer lay in the warmth and the brightness of the morning sunlight; in the sweetness of the morning wind. She put yesterday from her mind. *I will arise from my morning bed and go forth into the day. To the city will I go, to the canyons of the sun. Shower, spray and sparkle; needles on my skin. Rude awakenings are for those who gather dust in sad retreats and admit the myth of death.*

Down the street she walked in the morning shade of maples that sang sweet songs in the morning wind. At the station she caught the 9 :45, and early-afternoon found her in the city. However, she did not go directly to the Wilton as she had planned. She would go there later on, after he returned from the auction. That would be better than waiting for him in his room like a frightened little girl. After all, she knew her way around the city, didn't she? of course, quite well; thank you.

She stopped in a little restaurant and had a cheeseburger and a glass of milk, then she took in a double-feature matinee. The first feature was about a girl who found love on a south Pacific island. The second was about Moses. She liked them both very much. When she got outside, she found that it was night already. Well no, not really night; traces of daylight still lingered in the eastern sky. Just the same, she had no business being all alone in the big city at such an hour.

She remembered where the Wilton was, and hadn't the least trouble finding it. She had been there with her father once before. For years, the Dickensons had patronized it whenever business brought them to the city, and it had become traditional for the executives of DGM to patronize it, too. She remembered the lobby as a dignified room with thick rugs and big velvet armchairs. Now, even though the rugs and the chairs were still there, it seemed dingy and cheap, and somehow out of date. It was as though many years instead of only a few had passed since she had last been there.

The lobby was empty. So was the space behind the counter where the clerk should have been. Well, no matter, she knew were the register was kept. She would peek, that was what she would do. The name puzzled her for a moment when she first found it. It didn't seem quite right. And yet it must be. After it were the numerals 304.

An elevator bore her aloft, and soon she was walking down a carpeted hall. The carpet was frayed, and the walls were badly in need of paint. The door she wanted was at the very end. Just before she reached it, it opened, and a girl came out.

She was a bright-haired girl who looked as though she had just come off a production line where girls like herself were turned out like new Fords and Chevrolets. Elizabeth felt gawky and out of place just looking at her, and shrank back against the wall. When she thought of the moment in later years, she invariably pictured herself as a sort of anachronistic Emily Dickenson taken unawares by a neatly packaged product she had not dreamed existed, and perhaps, in the back of her mind where her little-girl masquerade had not taken effect, she pictured herself that way then, because the pattern must have begun somewhere, and at what more logical place could it have begun than at the beginning?

The girl did not look at her. As a matter of fact, she did not even see her. Elizabeth might just as well have been a painting hanging on the wall, a painting of a tall, thin girl with deceptively strong features and blue eyes that had in them the look of a bewildered child. But if the bright-haired girl did not see her, the man standing in the doorway of 304 did—the man who was—And yet wasn't—the man she had come to see. Gray-suited, concerned of countenance, the rouge-remnants of a kiss blazing brightly on his cheek, he stepped into the hall. "Elizabeth, I never dreamed you'd—" he began, and stopped. "Elizabeth, are you all right? You look strange."

The painting of Elizabeth Dickenson did not move.

Matthew paused helplessly before it. "Liz, this is one of those crazy things that happen to people when they're not looking," he said. "I saw the Wilton letterhead on some old correspondence at the shop and automatically took it for granted that it was a respectable place. I didn't find out that it had turned into a dive till after I'd registered and paid two days rent in advance. One of the bellboys told me then that no one from DGM has stayed here for years, but I decided to stick it out anyway. I—I never dreamed they'd send up a girl."

Still, the painting did not move.

"Come in, and sit down, Liz. You're as white as a ghost. This whole thing had no business happening to us—no business at all."

The painting turned back into an animate girl then, and the girl whirled, and ran down the hall. Matthew followed her to the elevator, argued desperately while it rose to her summons; and all the while, the smell of lipstick burned more and more vividly, When the elevator arrived, Elizabeth stepped inside and watched the closing doors devour his anguished face. Boarding the train for Sweet Clover all hour later, she left the little girl she once had been forever behind her.

*

The ship of the House of Dickens on, its doors closed tightly against the world, lay at anchor in the river of time.

Inside the house, young Elizabeth Dickenson sat in a wingback chair before a fireless fireplace. For the dozenth time that day, the phone rang. For the dozenth time, she let it ring.

After a while, it stopped; then it began ringing again. She went on sitting where she was.

Before her on a small footstool, a tray rested. On it were the remnants of the piece of toast she had had for breakfast, and a cup half full of cold coffee. The hour was 4: 16 P.M.; the day, the day after the day of the bright-haired girl.

Tires squealed in the driveway, the slam of a car door followed. The phone had finally fallen silent, and now, the doorbell commenced to ring. It rang and rang and rang. "I know it's you, Matt," Elizabeth whispered. "Go away—go away, please!"

Presently the ringing stopped, and the sound of the big brass knocker took over. Part of Elizabeth sprang to her feet, ran into the hall, and tried desperately to turn the knob that controlled the lock. But she was not strong enough. *Help me, help me!* she called to the rest of herself. *In a moment he'll be gone, and it'll be too late!*

The preponderance of herself did not move from the chair.

Are you going to let him go because what he did seemed twice as bad because you confused him with your father? Or are you going to let him, go because deep down in yourself you were looking for an excuse all along to shut yourself away front the world and write poetry?

Elizabeth Georgina Dickinson did not answer.

Presently the knocking stopped. A car door slammed. Once again, tires squealed.

Silence.

Elizabeth got up, went over to the Sheraton sofa table on which the phone stood, and dialed Curtis Hannock's office number. "This is Elizabeth Dickenson," she told the girl who answered. "Have you by any chance been. trying to get in touch with me today?"

"Why yes, Miss Dickenson. All afternoon, as a matter of fact. Hold the line a moment, please Mr. Hannock wants to speak with you."

"Elizabeth? Where in blazes have you been, girl?"

"It—it doesn't matter. What was it you wanted, Mr. Hannock?"

"To see you, of course, so that I can read you your father's will. How will it be if I drop around at two-thirty tomorrow afternoon?"

" . . . All right. Should I get in touch with anyone else?"

"No. It concerns you, and you alone. Two-thirty then—right? Take care of yourself, girl."

After hanging up, she stood for a while, staring at the wall. It was time to fix dinner, she supposed. She went out into the big kitchen and fried herself bacon and eggs and made a pot of coffee. The kitchen, with its plethora of modern appliances, was like another world—a world she didn't in the least appreciate. In remodeling it, Byron had gone all the way, but it could be said to his credit that he had junked none of the old equipment, some of which dated from Theodore Dickenson's day. Instead, he had stored it in the basement along with the various other period. pieces which both necessity and common sense had forced him to replace.

Dinner over, she washed the dishes, dried them and put them away. Afterward, she watched TV in the library with all the lights out, ignoring the occasional ringing of the phone. Once, the doorbell rang. She ignored that, too. At ten-thirty, she went to bed and lay dully in the darkness of her room. Toward three o'clock in the morning, exhaustion at last caught up to her, and she fell asleep.

Curtis Hannock showed up promptly at 2 :30 P.M. Thinning of hair, sharp of eye, he faced her across the big Chippendale table in the library. "Matt asked me to give you this," he said, tossing sealed envelope toward her, "and to tell you that if he doesn't get an answer, he won't bother you any more. Do you want to read it now, or would you rather wait till later?"

She let the envelope lie where it had fallen. "I'll wait till later."

"Very well." Hannock opened his brief case, spread out several papers on the table, and proceeded to read one of them. "All of which means," he said when he had finished, "that your father left you everything, or, to be more specific, the house and the factory. I'm sorry to say that his savings account is exhausted." Hannock raised his eyes. "Now, as to the house, there are no outstanding taxes, no mortgages, and the title seems to be clear enough, so you've no worries on that score. The factory, however, is a horse of a different nature."

"I want you to sell it," Elizabeth said.

"Hold your fire, now, girl. Wait till you hear the rest, and then make up your mind. Now, as you probably know, the plant's been in trouble for some time, and, as you probably also know, your father hired Matt in the hope of rejuvenating the place to a point where production would come somewhere near being on a par with other grain-machinery plants. But the trouble was, the company's finances wouldn't permit him to give Matt enough of a free hand, and although Matt's done the best anyone could have done under the circumstances, it hasn't been anywhere near enough. I advised your father to borrow the money that was needed for new equipment, but he wouldn't listen to me. I'd advise you to do the same, Elizabeth, and without the slightest hesitation; but fortunately I don't need to. After funeral expenses, and even after the bite which inheritance tax is going to take, the total of your father's life-insurance policies, of which you are the sole beneficiary and all of which contain double indemnity clauses, will be something like twenty thousand dollars. Sink every red cent of it into DGM girl—give Matt the free hand

he needs. Take my word for it, it's the soundest investment you can possibly make, and the best and the cheapest security you'll ever be able to buy. It's downright foolishness even to think of selling out!"

"That may be, Mr. Hannock, but I want to sell out just the same, and the sooner, the better. And I want whatever profit that accrues from the sale to be set up, along with the insurance money, in an annuity certain, and the payments credited to my checking account at the Sweet Clover National Bank."

Hannock's face grew red, and the nostrils of his thin nose quivered slightly, "Dammit, Elizabeth, you're a bright and intelligent girl. You could even run DGM yourself, if you had to, and with Matt working for you, you couldn't go wrong. Take my advice and hang on to the place and give him free rein. It'll give you a healthy interest in life and take you out of yourself. You're too withdrawn, girl—you've always been too withdrawn. And now you're going to go whole hog and pull out of the picture altogether. I don't know what Matt did to hurt you, but I'll bet it doesn't amount to a hill of beans and I'll bet you've magnified that hill into a mountain. Take it from me girl—forgive him. Forget about what he did, and then go on from there."

Elizabeth stood up. "I'm sorry, Mr. Hannock. I can't."

Sweeping his papers into his brief case, he got to his feet. "Matt'll probably quit, you know that, I suppose." Abruptly, he shrugged his shoulders. "I'll be in touch with you, girl."

THE HOUSE THAT TIME FORGOT

She accompanied him to the door. As he was about to depart, she touched his arm. "Will—will Matt be able to get another job all right?"

Hannock faced her. "It's kind of late in the day to be worried about that, isn't it?" Suddenly, pity came into his eyes. "Yes, yes, of course he'll be able to get another job." He turned away. "Take care of yourself, girl."

"Good by, Mr. Hannock."

After he drove off, she returned to the library. The envelope still lay on the Chippendale table. She looked at it for some time; then, resolutely, she picked it up, tore it into bits, and flung the bits into a nearby wastebasket. For a moment she thought she smelled smoke. It was an olfactory hallucination, of course, but in a sense the smoke was real. It was the smoke thrown out from the bridges that were burning behind her.

*

In the first month of her expatriation, Elizabeth ordered a marker for her father's grave. But she did not go near the grave even after the marker was ill place. Her groceries, she ordered over the phone. All of her bills, she paid by check, giving the letters to the mailman when he brought mail. She discontinued all of her magazine and newspaper subscriptions. She stopped listening to the radio. She no longer watched TV. Her contact with the world narrowed down to an occasional phone call from Curtis Hannock, an occasional letter (never answered) from one or another of her former acquaintances, an hello and a goodbye from the boy who delivered her groceries,. and the peripatetic gossip provided by Mrs. Barton, who still came biweekly to clean the house.

As more months passed, her days acquired a flexible routine. She would arise at six-thirty in the morning, fix breakfast, eat, tidy up the kitchen, and then return to her room and write poetry till noon. At noon, she would prepare herself a meager lunch, after which she would go outside and work on the grounds, operating her father's power-mower when the height of the grass warranted, trimming the hedge that effectively shutout the sight of the street, or weeding the small kitchen garden which she had planted next to the garage. Around four o'clock, she would go back inside and start preparing her evening meal. There were days, of course, when she fixed baked beans or a roast, and on these occasions the dish would have been put into the oven some hours before, making the preparation of the rest of the meal relatively simple. Evenings, she spent for the most part playing Bach or Couperin or Scarlatti on the harpsichord, becoming more and more proficient as the days passed. Sunday was her day off. She would arise at eight or eight-thirty, go downstairs, fix herself a light breakfast, and linger over a second and sometimes a third cup of coffee; then she would get whatever main course she had decided on for Sunday dinner into the oven, after which she would retire to the wing-back chair in the living room and read her bible until noon. She would eat dinner around one o'clock, do the dishes, and then go into the library, select a book, and retire once more to the wing-back chair. She read indiscriminately, choosing whatever volume her mood of the moment dictated, and most of the time she was in the process of reading half a dozen books at once. In this way she browsed through such diverse fare as *The Charterhouse of Parma, Moby Dick, Das Schloss, Little Men, Rebecca of Sunnybrook Farm, Ulysses,* and *Swann's Way.* Some of these literary pilgrimages she had made before, but all of them, new and old alike, provided her with the companionship which she was wise enough to know she could not get along without.

*

Summer faded into fall. Elizabeth was shocked when she got her school tax. The village tax had already bled her for $364.65, and now she was confronted with the prospect of being bled for $502.19 more. For a furious moment she was tempted to sell the house; then she remembered all the cherished old things it contained, and sold Byron's other car—a '61 Chrysler that was gathering dust in the garage—instead. Curtis Hannock took care of the transaction, and the price took care of the tax nicely and left her with a few hundred dollars to spare. She had Hannock set the amount aside for the state and county tax, which would show its ugly face come January 1st.

The first snow fell, and Elizabeth made arrangements to have her driveway kept open for the rest of the winter. Not that she expected company—her acquaintances had long since given up ringing her doorbell, and, while she had finally gone back to answering her phone, most of the calls she now received were "wrong numbers" but there was the grocery boy to be considered, not to mention the milkman and Mrs. Barton. The latter's "news-service" grew more and more extensive with each successive visit, and sometimes when the old woman got in the door Elizabeth despaired of ever getting her back out. *Item:* Amelia Kelly had just had another baby, which made four to date, and her husband not working and them living on his unemployment-insurance checks ! *Item:* The new owners of the Dickenson Grain-Machinery Company had shut down the factory till after the holidays, and all those poor employees with no money for Christmas! *Item:* Sid Westover, whose weather predictions had never been wrong yet, was down with lumbago again, so everybody might just as well resign themselves to a long, cold winter. *Item:* It was said that Matt Pearson, who had quit DGM when the new owners had taken over and returned to his home town to work in a new factory being opened there, was keeping steady company with his boyhood sweetheart, and any day now wedding bells were expected to ring. *Item:* Wasn't it just awful about the Gilbert boy running his father's car into the tail-end of a semi and killing himself? In the middle of January, Elizabeth paid the old woman off and told her that because of mounting taxes and the ever-climbing cost of living she had decided to economize by doing her own housework. "Humph!" Mrs. Barton said, and stamped out.

*

In mid-March, Elizabeth received a phone call from Curtis Hannock. He would have called sooner, he told her, but he had just heard the news himself: on March 4th, while helping to unload a vertical lathe at the ValleyVille branch of Fulcrum Industries, Inc., Matt Pearson had been crushed to death when the machine slipped off its rollers, overturned, and pinned him to the floor.

*

Let us take the years, the long and lonely years, and watch their slow, sad passage. There are two times—remember that. The time of the world and the time of the house—the present, and the past.

Elizabeth rising, Elizabeth dressing, Elizabeth descending the stairs. Elizabeth writing poetry, Elizabeth playing Bach, Elizabeth crying in her room at night . . .

Elizabeth Georgina Dickinson growing old.

The grounds, once so meticulously maintained, become more riotous with the passing of each spring. Paint peels from once-bright cornices and sills. Bricks darken with dampness and with grime. Each week, groceries are delivered, and deposited on back-porch steps that have seen far better days, there to be picked up by Elizabeth and taken hurriedly inside. Elizabeth no longer knows the sun or the rain; she runs at the sound of the milkman's tread, starts at the barking of dogs. Her only meetings with the night are the trips she takes in winter from the house to garage to bring in fireplace wood, two cords of which are split and delivered each year by a farmer she has never seen.

Nor has Elizabeth seen the city in which she lives. Oh yes, Sweet Clover is part of a city now. It was a part of a city before, although no one was aware of it—part of a vast megalopolis that spread all the way from Cleveland, Ohio to Buffalo, New York. Now, the megalopolis has come into its own and eaten Sweet Clover up, and all the green land around Sweet Clover, and the flowers and the trees. It would surprise Elizabeth to know that the farmer who delivers her cordwood is not in the strict sense of the word a farmer at all, but a "general supplier" who left his name with the "Bureau of Services" whose number "information" gave her when she dialed and asked where she might obtain wood to burn in her fireplace.

There is one thing, though, that Elizabeth knows: she knows that her property has tripled in value. Innumerable strange voices over the phone have importuned her to sell—in vain, of course—and her taxes have soared into the stratosphere. So high into the stratosphere, in fact, that it requires the better part of her income to pay them. She thinks that the house itself is responsible for this state of affairs, but she is wrong. The land on which the house stands is responsible. It is the only green land left in the city, and the city, officials want to buy it and turn it into a public park. It is perhaps better that Elizabeth does not know this, because turning the land into a public park would mean tearing down the house, and the house is her world. And then again, perhaps it would be better if she did know it. She might change her mind about dying intestate then, and see to it that her property falls into less iconoclastic hands. But in the long run, none of this will matter. In the long run, a slightly different scheme of things will exist, and no doubt the city will get its park without even half trying.

*

That fall, Elizabeth's school tax came to $1540.19. She scrimped for four months, but by the time she accumulated enough to pay it the state and county tax—now called the "megalopolis tax" came in with the amount of the unpaid school tax added on. The over-all amount was a demoralizing $2536.21.

Somehow, she had to raise the money. If she didn't, the next tax would put her so far behind that she would never be able to catch up. Her one contact with the world, Curtis Hannock, had been dead these many years, so she could not turn to him for help; and since her annuity was fixed, the only way she could raise money as far as she could see (other than by mortgaging the House of Dickenson, which was unthinkable) was by selling some of her possessions. The question boiled down to a matter of which of them she cared for least, and she had no trouble arriving at the answer: the "newest" ones, of course.

She took an inventory of the furniture, the appliances, the pictures, the dishes, the bric-abrac, and the books, jotting down the approximate age of each item. Then she made a chronological list, after which she grouped the items into general age-categories. They fell naturally into four groups: the "pre-Dickensonian" period, the "Theodore and Ann" period, the "Nelson and Nora" period, and the "Byron and herself" period. It went without saying that the latter group must be the first to be sacrificed.

She went through the house, inspecting each item individually. With rare exceptions, everything that she and her father had bought had by this time degenerated into junk. She had known of course that some of it was junk—the refrigerator, for one example, which had given up the ghost decades ago, and the television set, for another, which had conked out less than a year after the beginning of her expatriation and which she had never bothered to have fixed. But she had had no idea that the "modern" furniture had reached quite the sad state of affairs she found it in. Would she be able to get anything at all for such a sorry collection of keepsakes? she wondered. She would see.

"Seeing" involved doing something she had not done for years—coming face to face with another human being. But she had no choice, and when the collector to whom the Bureau of Services relayed her phoned request came around, she met him stanchly at the door. It is difficult to say which of them was the more taken aback. The collector saw a tall, gaunt woman, strong of features and silver of hair, clad in clothing that for an its immaculateness was at least half a century old. Elizabeth saw a short, pumpkin-bellied man, round of face and grass-green of hair, clad in a hair shirt with the hairside turned outward, leaf-green, calf-length trousers, and a pair of black shoes with long, snaky toes that brought to mind the roots of a small tree. In any event, it was the collector who recovered first. The minute Elizabeth ushered him into the living room, he headed straight for the harpsichord and said, "I'll buy this, two hundred dolla."

Elizabeth shook her head. "That isn't one of the items that's for sale. I'll show you those which you may buy."

She did so; conducting him from room to room, steering him away, with ever-increasing difficulty, from the Theodore-and-Ann and the Nelson-and-Nora pieces. When they got back to the living room, he said, "For the junk in the kitchen, two dolla, for the trash-furniture in this room, six dalla, for the pila books in the next room, ten dolla . . . For the harpsichord, two hundred dolla, for the Victorian, Sheraton, and Empire beds, two hundred dolla, for the copper-clock upstairs, fifty dolla, for the grandpop clock

27

downstairs, fifty dolla, for the Hepplewhite sideboard in the eating room, two hundred dolla, for the copper-strip bookcase in the hall, one hundred dolla—"

"But those pieces aren't for sale," Elizabeth objected. "Besides, the prices you're quoting are much too low."

The collector shrugged. "They're standard twenty-first century prices, lady. Antiques don't sell high-wise no more."

An inspiration struck Elizabeth. "I just remembered—there are some other things in the basement. Would you care to look at them?"

"Show me."

He offered her "one hundred dalla" for the lot, magnanimously exempting the an ancient pre-Dickensonian and ancient pre-Dickensonian sink, both of which he agreed to have his "haulaway boys" set up in the kitchen for her. The offer however, was contingent upon selling him the other items he had enumerated, plus a collection of Tarentum glassware which he has spotted in one of the kitchen cupboards. Elizabeth sighed. "I don't seem to have much choice, do I?" she said. She stood up straighter. "Very well—but the spool bed in my room is exempted, and I must have enough for the glassware to bring the over-all amount to a minimum of one thousand dolla—dollars. If you'd like I'll throw in the livingroom rug."

The collector made a face. "All right—one thousand dolla."

The house seemed naked after the "hollaway boys" had done their work and departed. There were poignant ellipses in furniture, empty and half empty rooms. The worst emptiness of all was the corner where the harpsichord had stood . . . Wearily, Elizabeth endorsed the check which the collector had left, made up the difference with a check of her own, and enclosed both checks in an envelope along with her tax receipts. She addressed the envelope, laid it along with a third check—this one for 20 cents to cover the postage—atop the mailbox outside the door, and weighted both items down with a small stone which she kept on hand for such purposes. The gas bill was due any day now, and when the mailman delivered it he would pick up the letter and mail it. She still thought of "him" as a "mailman," even though she knew that the purple-haired woman wearing the a yellow uniform that looked like a scuba outfit and riding a scooter-like cart now did the delivering. She had glimpsed her once through the hall window, put-putting up the walk, and once had been enough. Elizabeth seldom looked out her windows anyway. Even in the winter the trees and overgrown shrubs that surrounded the house effectively concealed the world that lay beyond her boundary lines, and that was as it should be. It was a world she wanted even lass part of than the world she had left behind her nearly half a century ago.

*

The idea of traveling into the past had never occurred to her, and it did not occur to her now in precisely those words. She merely noted as the days went that the house, bereft now of virtually all its tie-ins with the "future," had a new and refreshing flavor. This flavor grew on her, and to bring it out in greater purity she began carrying the various odds and ends that did not jibe with it out to the garage. Gradually this weeding-out process became an obsession with her, and hardly a night passed that she did not dispose of at least one "anachronistic object." she excepted the "modern" desk in her bedroom at which she still wrote her poetry, and there were, of course, certain aspects of the "future" that defied elimination. The "modern" electrical fixtures for example. The house had been wired in Nelson and Nora's day, but it had been rewired since, and none of the original fixtures remained. For a while she considered tearing the new ones out, but fortunately she still had enough common sense left to dissuade her, and she got around the incongruity by ordering a gross of candles and burning them instead of the electric lights. Some nights she would even dispense with candles, having discovered that she could read equally as well by firelight as she could by candlelight. Afterward, she would light a candle and climb the stairs to her room, pretending that the comfortable warmth of the house emanated, not from the automatic electric furnace which she herself had had installed circa 1990 when the gas furnace had breathed its last, but from the fire she had just left.

THE HOUSE THAT TIME FORGOT

Reading one February night in her wing-back chair, she became obsessed with the notion that all was not quite as it should be. Something in the house (aside from the writing desk in her room, the light fixtures and the telephone on the Sheraton sofa table) did not quite tie in with the Nelson-and-Nora atmosphere she had recreated. Her gaze roamed the shadows, lingered in this dark corner and that, and returned presently to the book lying on her lap. The name of it was *Bolts of Melody; New Poems of Emily Dickinson*. Surely the poems of Emily Dickinson belonged in the world of Nelson and Nora. Yes—generally speaking, they did; but these particular poems bore a 1945 copyright and had not previously been published. Therefor they did *not* belong. Even if they had belonged, the book itself wouldn't have. It would simply have to go.

So would the other books that Elizabeth had overlooked. There proved to be ten of them altogether. One by one she threw them into the fire. She saved *Bolts of Melody* till the last, and tears glistening evanescently on her cheek as she laid the treasured volume on the flames. The cover darkened, curled. The pages turned red, then black. Ashes rose like small gray ghosts, and drifted up the chimney—

Suddenly the house shuddered, and simultaneously the room filled with warm radiance. The light came from old-fashioned tasseled lamps and from a ridiculous chandelier consisting of painted cardboard candles with flame-like bulbs. In the empty spaces between the furniture, other furniture had appeared—furniture that matched the Nelson-and-Nora pieces and blended with the Theodore-and-Ann pieces; that went well with the lamps and the chandelier. The brown discoloration of the walls had been supplanted by flowery wallpaper; the once-lackluster woodwork gleamed. A young man sat reading a newspaper on a mohair sofa that a moment ago had not existed. A not-quite-so-young woman, bearing a tray on which stood a small teapot and two quaint cups, entered the room. Both the man and the woman wore clothing that dated from the early post-WW I period. Elizabeth stood transfixed, for the man was her grandfather and the woman was her grandmother—Nelson and Nora, happy in the home that was now theirs, the home they had just tastefully furnished with the new while still retaining the old.

The illusion—if illusion it was—faded away. Lights dimmed, went out, disappeared. The "new" furniture turned back into empty spaces; the walls resumed their brown discoloration, the woodwork lost its sheen. Nelson and Nora dissolved into empty air. It was as though a moment had come-and gone.

Looking at the walls, Elizabeth saw that the electrical fixtures were missing. Looking at the clock on the mantel, she saw that it had no hands.

She lit a candle and went through the downstairs rooms. None of the clocks had hands and some of them—the new ones which she had overlooked in her weeding-out operation—had disappeared. So had the cupboards that Byron had had built when he remodeled the kitchen. So had the inlaid linoleum on the kitchen floor. She went upstairs. So had the writing desk that contained every poem she had ever written.

At least her bed was still there, and her sheets and blankets and pillows. The bed, being pre-Dickensonian, would have been exempt in any case, but the sheets and blankets and pillows were relatively new. Maybe what had happened to the house had affected only those articles that were an integral part of the house. Frightened, broken-hearted, she undressed and slipped beneath the covers. She blew out the candle and closed her eyes. Lying there, she tried to reassure herself. She had been living alone too long—that was it. She had let her obsession with the past get the best of her common sense. In the morning, her common sense would be back at the helm, and everything would be back to normal again.

But morning did not come.

She could not believe it at first when she awoke to total darkness. She had slept for at least eight hours, and daybreak should have been on hand. She lit her candle, got out of bed, and went over to the window. Blackness lay beyond the panes, blackness unrelieved by the faintest gleam or sparkle or particle of light.

Standing there, she became aware of the intense cold. Had the furnace gone out? Slipping into her blue dressing gown, she hurried downstairs. The living room was like an ice box, the kitchen was like a deepfreeze. Holding her candle before her, she descended the basement stairs. The electric furnace had vanished. So had the electric hot-water tank. So had the water pipes and the wiring.

Well anyway, her teakettle was full.

She was trembling now, partly from fright, but mostly from the cold. Returning to the kitchen, she built a fire in the wood stove and when it was going good she went into the living room and built another one in the fireplace. As warmth rose around her, some of her confidence returned. Remembering that there was snow on the ground, she found a pan in the kitchen and stepped out onto the back porch. Instantly, the candlelight shrank into a tiny sphere of wan light and she found that she couldn't see beyond a radius of two feet. The cold was unbearable, the blackness terrifying. She had a sudden, horrible conviction that the house no longer rested on solid earth and that if she were to step down from the porch, she would step into nothingness. Shuddering, she went back into the kitchen and closed the door.

The cordwood, she thought numbly. *If I can't get to the garage, how am I going to keep my fires going?*

There could be only one answer, and presently it came to' her: *By burning the furniture.*

Thus far, she had not reacted to the situation the way a normal person would have reacted. Living alone for so long, she had failed to consider the possibility that the catastrophe that had overtaken her might have overtaken others as well, that it might, in fact, have overtaken the entire world. When the thought finally occurred to her, she hurried back into the living room, hungry for the first time in years for the sound of a human voice. However, her hunger was not appeased. There wasn't even an outline in the dust on the Sheraton sofa table to show where the phone had been. She stood very still and clenched her hands into fists. "I won't scream," she said. "I won't."

Maybe somewhere in the house there was a transistor radio which she might have overlooked and which might still have enough power in its batteries to enable her to pick up a nearby station. It was a bright and shining hope while it lasted, but it didn't last long. She knew without even having to think that if there had been such a radio, it no longer existed any more than the phone did, any more than anything else that was endemic to the house and in the least incongruous with the Nelson-and-Nora period. Besides, even if one did exist and even if its batteries still had power in them, what good would it be to her? Radio waves couldn't penetrate where light waves couldn't

.

Penetrate? Penetrate what? She frowned, trying to think. Did she understand unconsciously what had happened and was her unconscious mind reluctant to release the facts because they were too unpleasant? She closed her eyes. Maybe she could visualize the situation symbolically. At first, she "saw" nothing.

Then, gradually, a river took form. It was a wide river, flowing evenly between indeterminate banks, and in the middle of it there was a large rock. The part of the rock that rose above the surface was damp, indicating that the river had recently washed over it, and then leveled off. Elizabeth waited for more details to manifest themselves, but the image remained the way it was. At length she opened her eyes, no wiser than she had been before.

The fire was dying down, and she added more wood. She remembered that she hadn't had breakfast yet, and went into the kitchen and made a small pot of coffee. Raising one of the grids of the ancient wood stove, she toasted a slice of bread over the flames. She had enough food on hand to keep her going for a week—two, if she rationed it—and there were a couple of dozen quarts of fruit juice with which she could eke out her water supply. Of course she couldn't make coffee with fruit juice, but it wouldn't hurt her to go without coffee. "Why am I thinking like this?" she asked herself suddenly. "I act as though it really matters whether I live or die."

That afternoon, she found an ancient hatchet in the basement, brought it upstairs, and began breaking up enough furniture to see her through the night. As always, she saved the old at the expense of the new, and when she decided to supplement her fuel supply with books, the ones she brought in from the library were, like the furniture, directly related to the Nelson-and-Nora period.

She hesitated over Emily Dickinson's *Further Poems*, but ultimately decided that it, too, must go, and piled it with the other doomed volumes.

She looked at the wing-back chair and the footstool. She would never burn them. Nor would she ever burn the bed in her room. The three pieces, along with the handless clock on the mantel and the wood stove in the kitchen, were the oldest items in the house. They *Were* the house, in away . . .

The books and the broken-up furniture stacked neatly beside the fireplace, Elizabeth fixed herself a frugal dinner. Afterward, she settled down before the fire with *Sonnets by E.B.B.* She spent the "night" in the wing-back chair, augmenting the heat from the fire, to which she periodically added books and wood, with a yellow lap robe. The cold neither intensified nor lessened. There was no wind, or if there was, she could not hear it; no sound at all save for the crackling of the flames. When she thought it was morning, she went out into the kitchen and fixed breakfast. During the next three "waking periods," as she came to call them, she broke up the rest of the Nelson-and-Nora furniture and burned it along with the Nelson-and-Nora books. It was with a feeling of vast regret that she cast the last volume into the flames. She felt as though she was destroying an entire age, a whole way of life; and the destruction was made all the more poignant by the fact that the last volume was Emily Dickinson's *The Single Hound*.

She watched the cover curl, saw the pages blacken. *Words, words,* she thought. *Your life, like mine, Emily, was words, words, words—words written in our lonely rooms, in secret and in silence and in pain, while without our windows birds sang, and lovers walked beneath the trees. Oh Matt, Matt, words are not enough to fill a person's life; as sustenance, they feed the soul, but starve the heart; and the patterns that we form with them are patterns, and nothing more. Pointless patterns falling like the leaves of life upon the dusty lap of death.*

The pages crinkled, turned to ashes; the cover crumbled away. The flames died down, and the room darkened . . . then grew abruptly bright with gaslight as the House of Dickenson shuddered. A Victorian side table with a marble top materialized along an empty wall. On it stood a Gothic wax light. In a poignant corner, a familiar harpsichord appeared. Gaily-patterned hooked rugs came into being on the barren floor. A fantastic chandelier appeared hanging from the suddenly immaculate ceiling, and walls and woodwork took on a brighter hue. A Victorian rosewood sofa sprang into existence where only dust and desuetude had been, and on it sat a young woman in a gay-nineties dress, crocheting in the radiance of a Pickle-jar lamp. Tantalizing aromas emanated from the kitchen, and somewhere in the house a music box was playing Brahm's *Lullaby*.

The moment was as transient as the first moment had been. In a sense, it was a picture glimpsed while riffling through the pages of a book. Now, the pages had come together, and the room was as it had been before, shadow-filled, pale with the radiance of fainting flames, inhabited only by an old woman sitting in a wing-back chair—an old woman whose resurrected spectacles did little for her fading vision, but who nevertheless had peered back through the pages of time and seen her own great-grandmother.

Half dreaming, half awake, Elizabeth became aware of the awesome cold that had crept into the room. It was time to break up the rest of the furniture; time to burn the rest of the books.

She broke up all of the remaining pieces, all except the wingback chair, the footstool, and her bed, and piled the remaining books by the fireplace, exempting only *Sonnets by E.B.B.* She wound the clock on the mantel in order that she might hear its rhythmic voice. "Tick-tock, ticktock," it said, and chimed the hour of nothing.

The third and final shudder came two "waking periods" later while the fire was burning bright and nothing remained to be consumed but the remnants of a Chippendale highboy. This time, there was no sudden brightness, only a gradual paling of the shadows as twilight tiptoed into the room. Going to the front door, Elizabeth opened it and looked out.

THE HOUSE THAT TIME FORGOT

Night was falling swiftly. However, there was still enough light to see by. Upon the ground, snow lay; but it wasn't the same snow that had lain there before. Nor was the ground quite the same. The trees, too, had changed, and the shrubbery had disappeared. As for the street, it was a street no more, but a country road. Across it rose a stand of basswoods; some distance down it the buildings of a small village showed. Elizabeth heard the sound of sleigh-bells. She knew who she was then, who she had been all along. *Before I was born, I died, she thought. Before I knew the light of day, I breathed the breath of night. My sun had already set before I even saw it. And it was I and I alone who instigated this travesty of time.*

She stepped back into the House of Death and closed the door behind her. She listened in the silence, and presently she heard their wings. She was glad that they had come.

*

What is a generation-house if it is not the sum of the generations that have lived in it, and what is that sum if it is not the sum of the possessions those generations have left behind? Let us take the quantity "8" and assume that it has been arrived at by the following process:

2+2=4; 4+2=6; 6+2=8

In the case of the House of Dickenson, there had been the time of Theodore, the time of Nelson, the time of Byron, and before those times there had been the time of the old woman in the wing-back chair. Let the time of the old woman equal 2, the time of Theodore equal 4, the time of Nelson equal 6, and the time of Byron equal 8. Now, the sum of a tree is the number of its rings, and by those rings, its years can be computed. It follows logically that if those rings could be removed one by one, the tree would grow progressively younger. In the case of a tree, this is manifestly impossible; but a generation-house is not a tree. The "rings" of a generation-house are the marks left by the people who have lived in it—the chairs and the sofas and the clocks and the books which those people left behind. Such "rings" as these *can* be removed, not entirely perhaps, but to an extent where the "ring" loses its identity and ceases to be; and if the house is ideally constituted, the forces

36

of time themselves can be fooled. Now, let us reverse the process used to obtain 8:

8-2=6; 6-2=4; 4-2=2

Consider: What binds a composite object such as a generation-house to present? Is it not the presence in that house of objects belonging to the present? Is it not the presence of people in that house who *live* in the present? When a house is abandoned and allowed to fall into desuetude, it eventually acquires the reputation of being haunted, does it not? And because of this do we not consider it as being detrimental to our neighborhood and start taking the necessary steps to get rid of it? Thus do we cooperate with the forces of time, for the forces of time do not like abandoned houses either. Such houses are too easy to forget, and they are haunted in order that our attention will be drawn to them. Moreover, they are haunted; not by apparitions out of the past, but by apparitions out of the future; by the supernatural minions of time.

There are cases, however, when a house loses its tie-in with the present without being abandoned, and this is the kind of house that the forces of time invariably forget. Once forgotten, the house slips back into a more appropriate moment, conforms completely to that moment, and remains in abeyance till that moment passes; then the time-paradox factor goes into action and the house is automatically relegated to a timeless limbo where, in ordinary cases, it remains forever, all memory of it wiped from the minds of men. But the House of Dickenson did not constitute an ordinary case: owing to the individual character of its "rings" and to the precision with which they were removed, it slipped back into the past, not once, but three times, and on the third occasion it outraged the laws of cause and effect by precluding its own beginning. At this point, the forces of time awoke to the fact that a cycle had been set in motion underneath their very proboscides, and they dispatched their minions to eliminate it. The trick was to make 2= 8, thereby forcing the law of probabilities to cause Theodore to build the house, and to cause the original contents of the house to be acquired at a later date. The key factor was an old woman sleeping in a wing-back chair.

THE HOUSE THAT TIME FORGOT

*

Opening her eyes, old Elizabeth Dickenson glimpsed lavender flutterings in the firelit room. "Come," she said impatiently. "Do what you have to do, and have done with it. Why do you keep an old woman waiting?"

Silence, then the dismal *flap-flap* of leathery wings. Elizabeth dozed again. Beside her, the flames crackled briskly as they consumed the last of the Chippendale highboy. Something cold and silken touched her cheek, but she neither stirred, nor opened her eyes. "Dress me in my burial gown if you must," she murmured. "Hang the grave damps round my head. But get on with your loathsome business."

The flapping crescendoed. There was a soporific quality about it. "I'm sorry, Matt," she whispered. "Unknowingly I held your life in my hands. Unknowingly I let you die." She sank down deeper into the chair. It was warm and restful there. *Now I lay me down to sleep,! pray the obbly-gobblies my soul to keep. And if I die before I wake, I pray the obbly-gobblies my soul to take—*

There was a knocking at the door.

The clatter of brass striking upon brass.

Young Elizabeth Dickenson opened her eyes.

A silvery web encased both her and the wing-back chair she sat in. She brushed the web away, and it was like wiping film from her eyes. The clock on the mantel said 4 :19.

Matt, she thought. Matt, come to apologize. Part of her sprang to her feet, ran into the hall, and tried desperately to turn the knob that controlled the lock. But she was not strong enough. *Help me, help me!* she called to the rest of herself. *In a moment he'll be gone, and it'll be too late!*

Elizabeth did not move.

Suddenly a vista of long and empty years opened in her mind; long and empty years leading down, down, back, back, into darkness, into cold. She saw an old woman sitting by a fire. She saw two winged and hideous shapes.

Still, she did not move.

The image of the old woman faded from her mind, and the image of a man lying crushed beneath a ponderous machine took its place. "Matt, no!"

She was on her feet then, and running into the hall. She tore wildly at the knob, threw open the door. He was standing there in the late-afternoon sunlight, eyes hungry for the sight of her. In a moment, she was in his arms—

The face of all the world is changed, I think,
Since first I heard the footsteps of thy soul . . .

www.ingramcontent.com/pod-product-compliance
Lightning Source LLC
Chambersburg PA
CBHW050909120626
46554CB00003B/1098